Kevin Crossley-Holland

The Ugly Duckling

from the story by Hans Christian Andersen

Illustrated by Meilo So

Orion
Children's Books

How lovely it was in the summer country! Green oats, and wheat green-and-gold; the thick sweet smell of newly-scythed hay.

The storks went walking on their long red legs through the shining fields and the sunlight settled on the shoulders of the ancient castle. It winked in the moat. It warmed all the outstretched hands of the burdocks that grew so thick and tall you could walk under them and pretend you were in the middle of the forest.

And amongst these burdocks, between the castle and the moat, a duck had built her nest.

One by one her eggs cracked; one by one, little heads poked out, little eyes blinked, little beaks opened. 'Peep!' they said. 'Peep!'

'Quack!' said their mother. 'Look around you!'
So the ducklings blinked at the green world, and the green was good for their eyesight.

'How large the world is!' peeped the baby ducklings.

'Large!' said the mother. 'You haven't seen half of it. It stretches as far as Church Meadow.' When the duck stood up, she saw one of her eggs – the biggest one – had still not hatched. 'Bother!' she said. 'How much longer? I'd like to go for a swim.'

Then one of the old ducks came flouncing through the burdock to visit her.

'Look at them!' said the mother duck. 'Aren't they the sweetest things you ever saw? But one egg won't hatch.'

'Let me have a look at it,' said the old duck. 'Yes, that's a turkey's egg. You won't want to bother with that. Turkey chicks won't even go near the water.'

'I'll sit on it just a little longer,' said the duck.

'It's up to you!' said the old duck, and she flounced off through the burdock.

At last the big egg cracked open and the chick fell out.

'Peep! Peep!' he said. He was very large and very ugly.

'He doesn't look like the others at all,' said the mother duck.
'I wonder if he really is a baby turkey.'

But when the mother duck took her babies down to the moat,
she didn't have to nip or kick the ugly duckling to get him into the water.

'He's not a turkey,' she said. 'He knows what to do with his legs. He holds his
neck up straight. He's my own baby. In fact,' she said, 'if you look at him carefully,
he's rather handsome.'

Later that day, the duck led her family to the henyard to meet everyone.

'Keep close to me,' she said, 'and then no one will step on you. And watch out for the cat!'

In the henyard, two families of ducks were pecking and squabbling over an eel's head. But neither of them got it! The cat pounced on it.

'That's how life is,' the mother duck told her ducklings. 'Quack! Don't walk! Waddle properly – keep your legs well apart, like I do. And now,' she said, 'come with me. You must bow to the old duck.'

But then other ducks began to gather round the mother duck and her
little family.

'We don't want this bunch, do we?'

'There's enough of us here already.'

'Look at the ugly one! We're not having him.'

Then one duck actually bit the ugly duckling on the neck. 'Leave him alone!' the mother duck shouted. 'He hasn't harmed you.'

'He's too big,' said the biter-duck. 'He's not like anyone else. Isn't that good enough reason?'

'What lovely little children!' said the old duck. 'All except one.'

'He's ever so obliging, my lady,' said the mother duck. 'And he can swim just as well as the others. In fact, even a little better.'

'Well, the other ones are pretty,' the old duck said. 'Make yourselves comfortable.'

But the poor little duckling was jostled and bitten by the other ducks and even by the hens. The turkey cock gobbled at him until he was red in the face. The sad little creature wished he were not so ugly, and didn't know where to hide.

And this was just the first day; every day was worse than the one before.
The poor duckling was even chased around by his own brothers and
sisters, and they kept quacking, 'You ugly creature! If only the cat would get you!'
The ducks bit him. The hens pecked him. The hen girl kicked him. And finally
even his mother said, 'I wish you weren't here – I wish you were a long way away.'

Then the duckling ran away. He flew a long way away until he reached a great marsh where wild ducks lived, and he was so tired he stayed there for the night.

Next morning, the wild ducks discovered him.

'What sort of bird are you?' asked one.

'You're certainly ugly,' said another. 'But what does that matter?'

The ugly duckling spent two days in the marsh, swimming amongst the reeds, sipping water.

Then two wild geese – two young ganders – flew up to him.
'Listen, mate!' they said. 'You're so ugly we rather like you.
Do you want to come with us? Come on!'

'Bang! Bang!'
The two young ganders fell into the reeds, dead; the water turned red around them.

'Bang! Bang!' The whole marsh was surrounded by guns. Guns in the bushes; guns amongst the reeds, guns in the trees, a great skein of wild geese started up.

There was blue smoke over the marsh, and the sound of splashing dogs.

The poor little duckling was terrified. Just as he was tucking his head under his wing, so as to hide himself, he saw a large dog eyeing him through the reeds. The dog's tongue was hanging out and it bared its teeth. But . . . then splash! splash! It just turned away.

'Mercy!' cheeped the little duckling. 'I'm so ugly not even the dog wants me.'

The shooting went on all day, and it was hours before the frightened little duckling dared raise his head from under his wing. Then he ran away. He scooted out of the marsh, and across the fields, fighting his way into the wind.

At dusk, the ugly duckling spied a crooked little hut. An old woman lived in it with her cat, who could arch his back and purr, and make sparks if you stroked his fur in the wrong direction, and her hen, who laid lots of eggs.

In the dark, the duckling squeezed into the hut through the crack where the door had come off one of its hinges and next morning the cat and hen discovered him.

'Aha!' said the woman. 'We're in luck! We'll have eggs before long, unless it's a drake.'

The duckling stayed in the hut for three weeks, but of course he laid no eggs.
And the cat and the hen, who thought they knew everything, scarcely let the
duckling open his mouth.

'Can't you lay eggs?' asked the hen.
'No,' said the duckling.
'Shut up, then!'

'Can you arch your back?' asked the cat. 'Do you know how to purr?
Or make sparks?'
'No.'
'In that case, you're not worth listening to.'

But when the duckling started to think about fresh air and sunlight, he so longed to go swimming he couldn't bear not to talk about it.

'Swimming! What a ridiculous idea!' said the hen. 'If you could lay eggs, or purr, you'd soon forget about swimming.'

'It's so lovely to float on the water,' said the duckling, 'and wet your head, and dive to the bottom.'

'So lovely,' said the hen. 'I think you've gone mad. Quite mad!'

'You don't understand,' cried the duckling.

'Don't understand, don't I?' said the hen. 'The cat and I understand a great deal more than you ever will. It's time you did something useful.'

'No,' said the duckling. 'I'm going to see the wide world for myself.'

'You do that!' said the hen.

So the duckling left the hut. He walked and he flew until he came to a lake where he could float and dive to the bottom. The other ducks turned their backs on him because he was so ugly.

Autumn came and the yellow and brown leaves danced in the wind; winter followed and the clouds sagged with snow and hail. 'Ow! Ow!' croaked a raven perched on a fence. 'Ow! Cold!'

One day, as the winter sun set in a flood of fire, a flock of the most beautiful birds floated out of the rushes. Their feathers were shining white; their necks were long and graceful; they were swans. The swans whooped, and beat their strong, stately wings, they climbed and circled, and the ugly duckling spun round and round in the water like a wheel, and reached out for the sky, and cried with longing.

Then the swans flew way south to a warmer country, and the duckling dived
to the bottom of the lake. He was so miserable. He knew he loved these birds far
more than he had ever loved anyone before; and he didn't know where they had
gone to. He didn't even know their names.

It grew cold and then even colder. The ice on the lake muttered and groaned
and the duckling had to swim round and round to keep his little water hole open.
But each night his space became smaller and in the end he was too worn out to
swim any longer. The ice closed round him and locked him in.

Next morning, a farmer found the duckling. He kicked away the ice around him, and freed him; he put him under one arm and took him back to his wife.

The duckling was so scared of the farmer's playful children that he spread his wings and splashed straight into the milk pail – from there, he blundered into the butter churn, and then he flapped into the flour barrel.

The farmer's wife was furious. She shouted at the duckling and chased him with a poker, and the duckling flew out of the farmhouse door. He lay under some bushes, in a little drift of snow.

That was a terrible winter for the duckling. All the same, he managed to survive, and one morning he felt the sun shine warmly on his back. Spring had come again.

Then the duckling spread his wings – they were so strong now and stately. He climbed and he flew and, far from the lake, he saw a lovely garden. The apple-trees there were in blossom, and lilac bushes bent low over a winding canal.

Then out of the reeds floated three swans. They ruffled their feathers; they sat so lightly on the water, and for a second time the duckling was filled with a deep sadness.

'They're royal birds,' he said, 'and I'll fly down to them. And if they tear me to pieces because I'm so ugly, or because I tried to speak to them . . .Well, I'd rather that than be bitten by ducks, and pecked by hens, and kicked by the hen-girl, and frozen by the bitter cold.'

So the duckling flew down to the water. He swam towards the royal swans. And the swans turned to meet him.

The poor thing lowered his head and stared into the water, and waited for the swans to peck him and kill him. But what did he see? He saw he was no longer grey and gangling, no longer graceless or awkward or ugly. He was a swan!

The three swans encircled him and gently nuzzled him with their beaks.

Some children came down to the canal with bread for the swans.
'Look! There's a new one!' shouted the youngest, and they
all hared back indoors to tell their parents.

Then the whole family fed the swans with bread and cake, and they all agreed the new one was the loveliest of all. The older swans kept bowing to him.

The new young swan felt very shy, and he tucked his head under one wing. He was happy, so happy. The white and purple lilac bent right down to the water for him. The sun shone warmly for him. He ruffled his feathers; he arched his slender neck.

'I never knew,' he said. 'When I was the ugly duckling,
I never knew there was such happiness as this.'